For the fathers and the sons
—A.D.

For Rudolph "Tito" Gutierrez,
my father, my friend, my hero,
Mr. Fantastic
—R.G.

Library of Congress Cataloging-in-Publication Data
Dorros, Arthur.
    Papá and me / by Arthur Dorros ; illustrated by Rudy Gutierrez. — 1st ed.
       p.   cm.
    Summary: A bilingual boy and his father, who only speaks Spanish, spend
a day together.
    ISBN 978-0-06-058156-5 (trade bdg.) — ISBN 978-0-06-058157-2 (lib. bdg.)
    [1. Fathers and sons—Fiction. 2. Bilingualism—Fiction. 3. Hispanic
Americans—Fiction.] I. Gutierrez, Rudy, ill. II. Title.
PZ7.D7294Pap 2008   2007011868
[E]—dc22

Typography by Dana Fritts
3 4 5 6 7 8 9 10

First Edition

Arthur Dorros

Papá and Me

PICTURES BY **Rudy Gutierrez**

rayo

An Imprint of **HarperCollinsPublishers**

"**Good morning!**" I call to Papá.

"*Buenos días,*" Papá says back to me.

He pushes sleep from his eyes.

I am awake and ready to go.

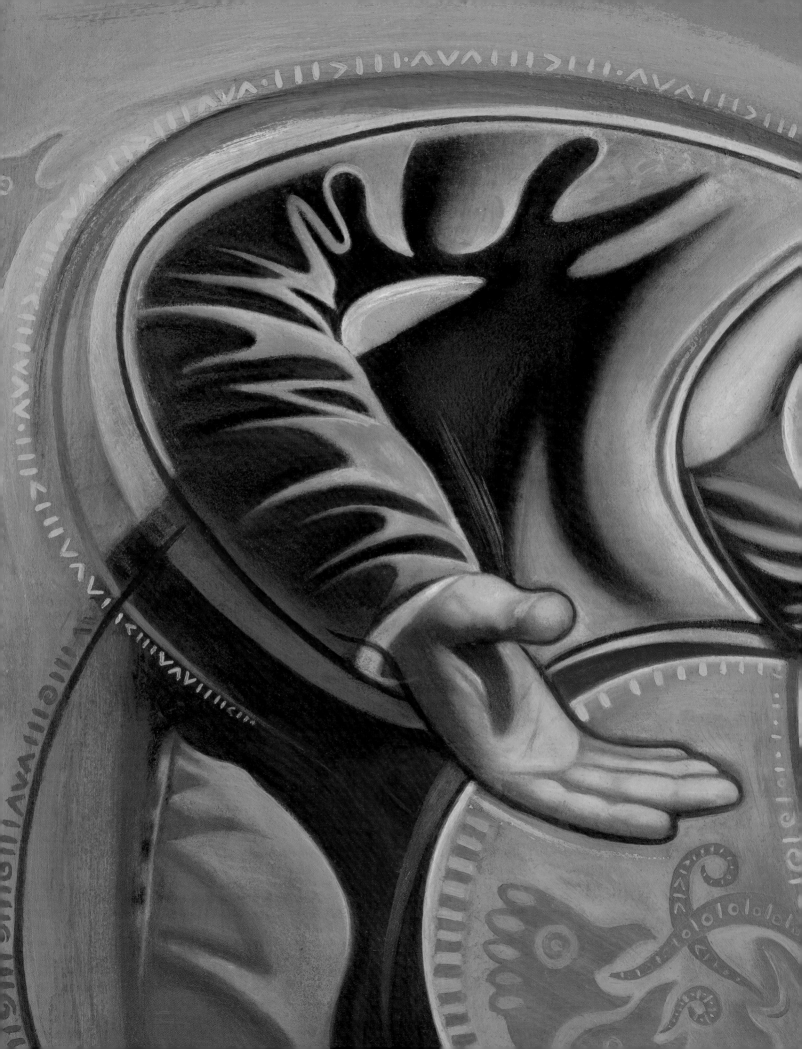

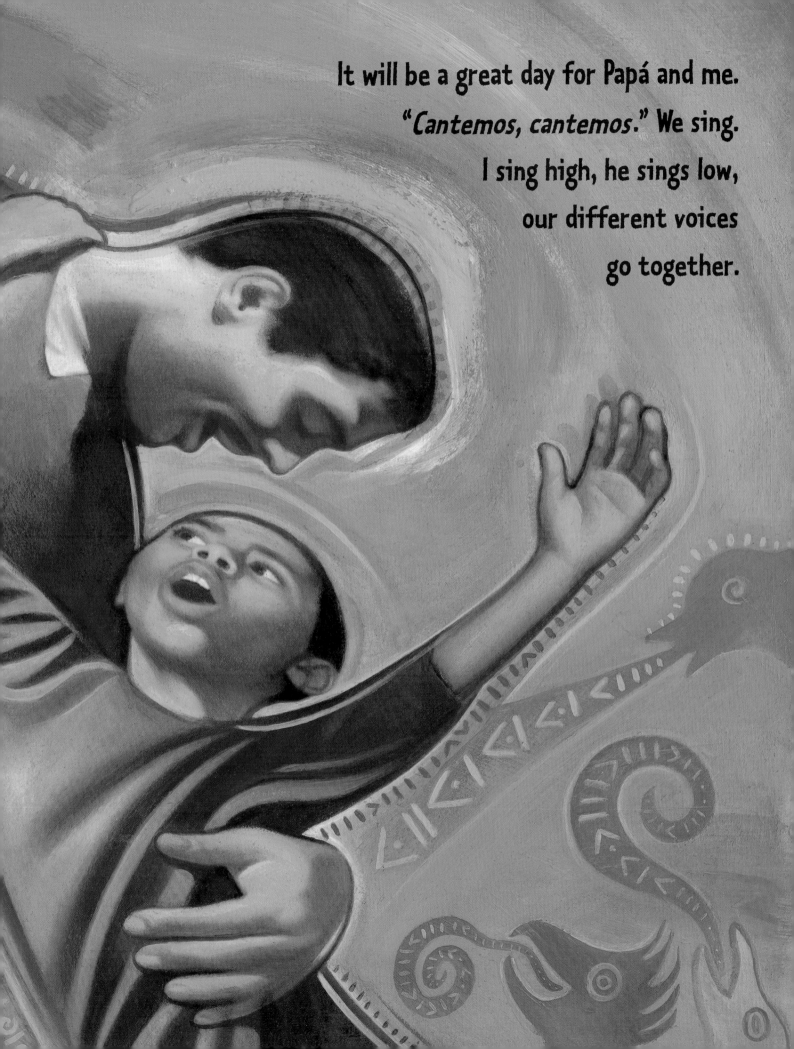

It will be a great day for Papá and me.
"*Cantemos, cantemos.*" We sing.
I sing high, he sings low,
our different voices
go together.

We are always cooking up something new.

He wants eggs. I say pancakes!

Papá brings down a plate.

He flips, I catch.

We invent a special food.

"*¡Sabroso!*" Papá says it is so tasty.

Today I know just where to go.
Crossing the street, Papá says,
"*La mano*," and takes my hand.
I have an idea. Papá has an idea too.

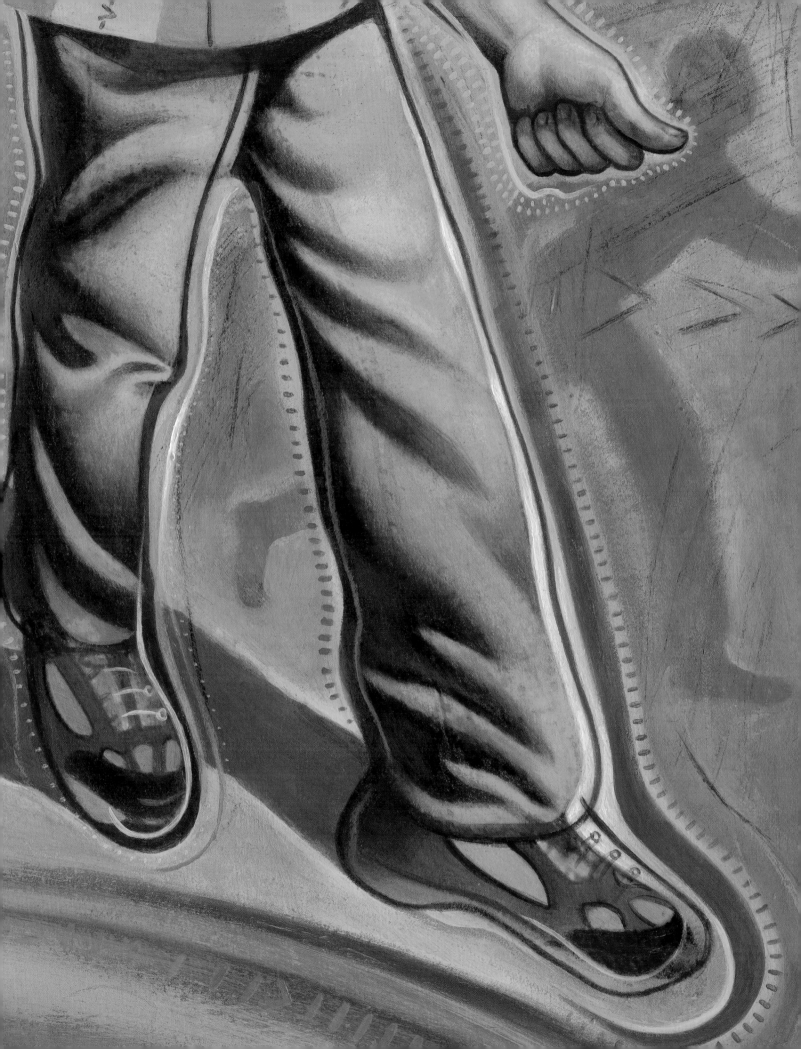

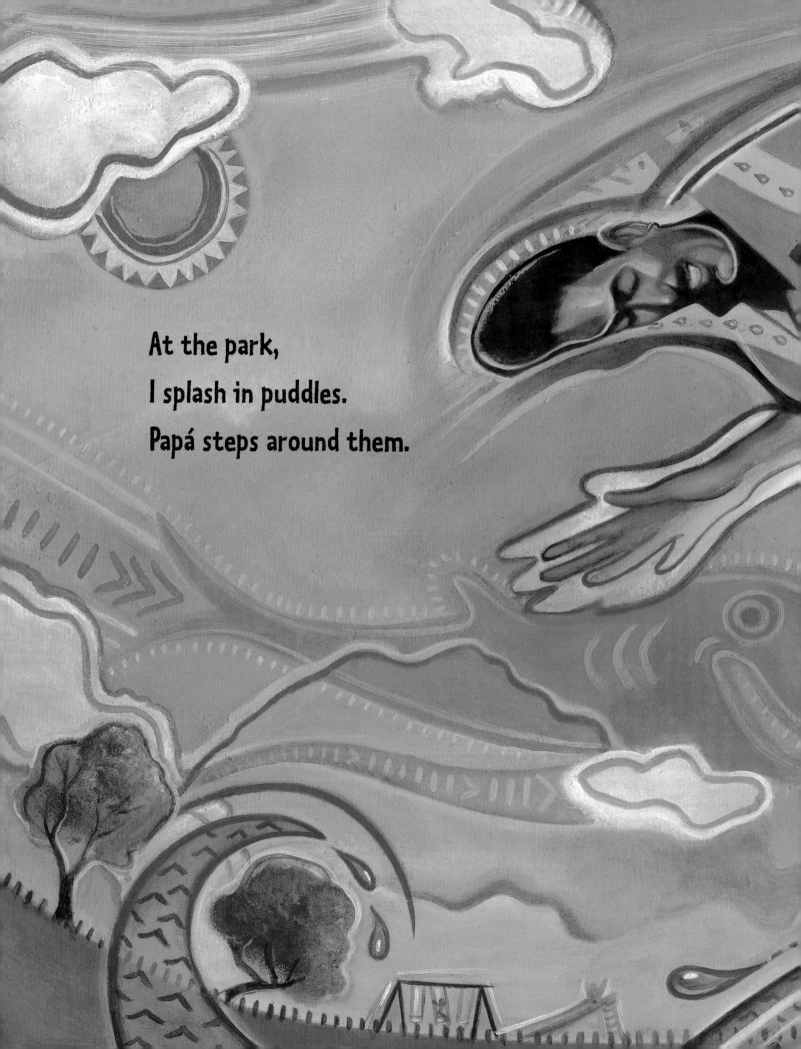

At the park,
I splash in puddles.
Papá steps around them.

"*Agua Man*."

"Water Man" he calls me.

Water here, water everywhere.

Papá swings me over.

There's a tree I want to climb.

I can't reach the branches.

Papá boosts me.

"*Alto, alto,* high!" I say.

I sway with the wind,

showing Papá what I can do.

I am flying, flying.

"*Cuidado.*" Be careful, Papá says to me.

"*Mira*, look," I tell him.

A bird is up there.

"*Águila.*" Eagle, Papá tells me.

He says my eyes see things he can't see.

In the sand,
I draw Papá's face. *"La cara,"*
he says, and draws me.

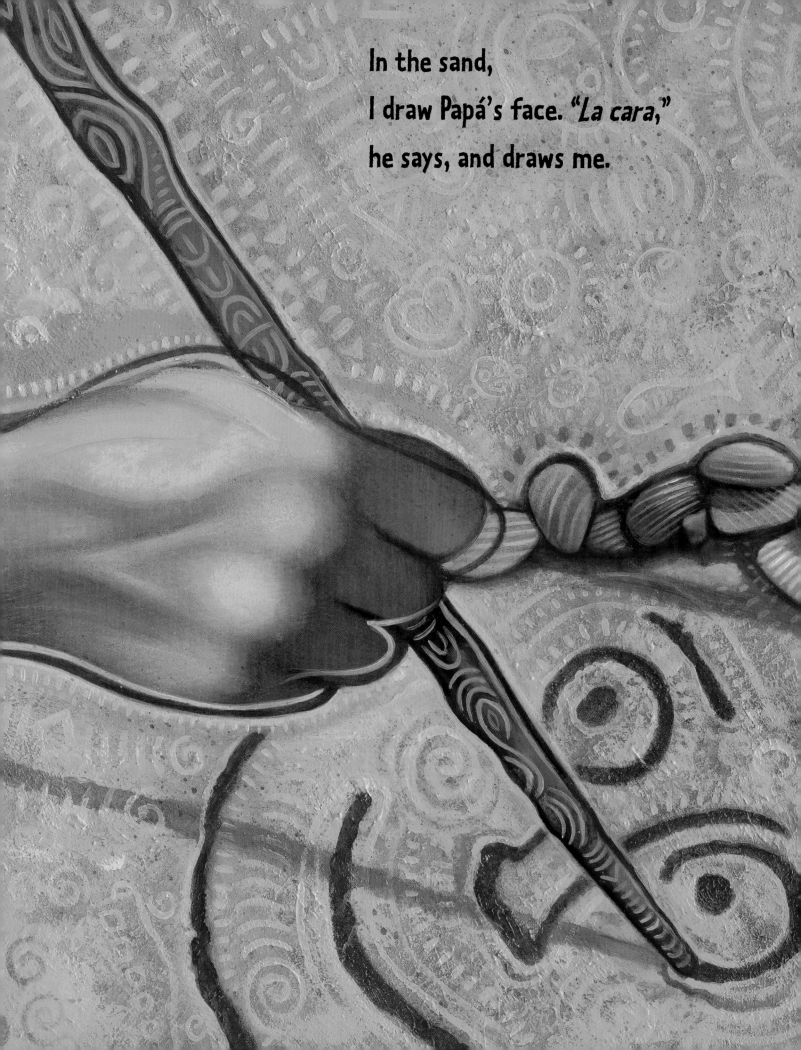

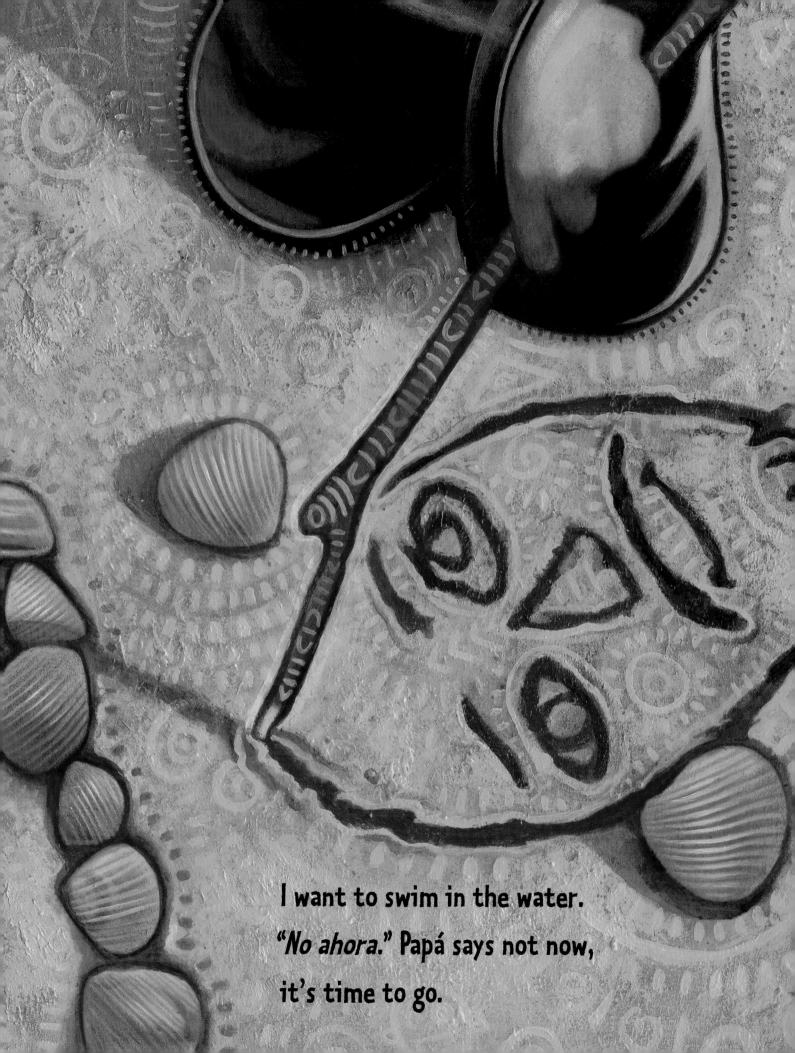

I want to swim in the water.

"No ahora." Papá says not now,

it's time to go.

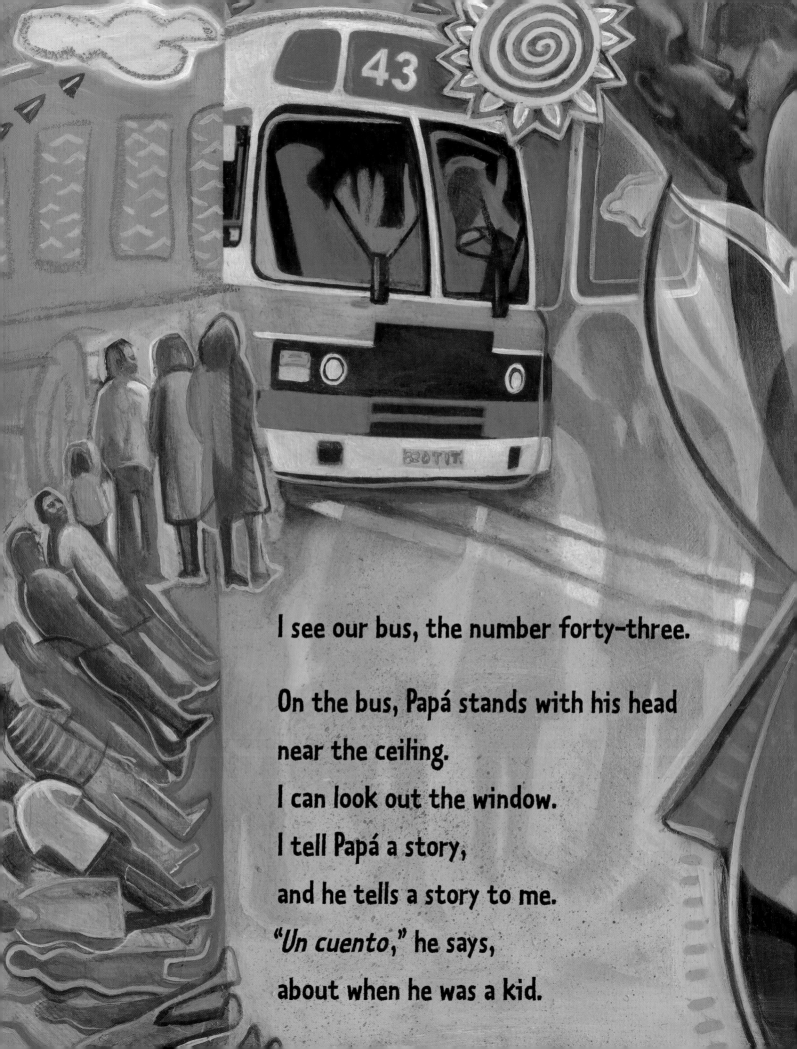

I see our bus, the number forty-three.

On the bus, Papá stands with his head
near the ceiling.
I can look out the window.
I tell Papá a story,
and he tells a story to me.
"*Un cuento*," he says,
about when he was a kid.

"Our stop, our stop!" I say to Papá.
I push the button and the bus
slows down.

Papá and me race the rest of the way.
I can do some things better than Papá,
he can do some better than me.

"¡Ganador!"

"¡Ganador!"

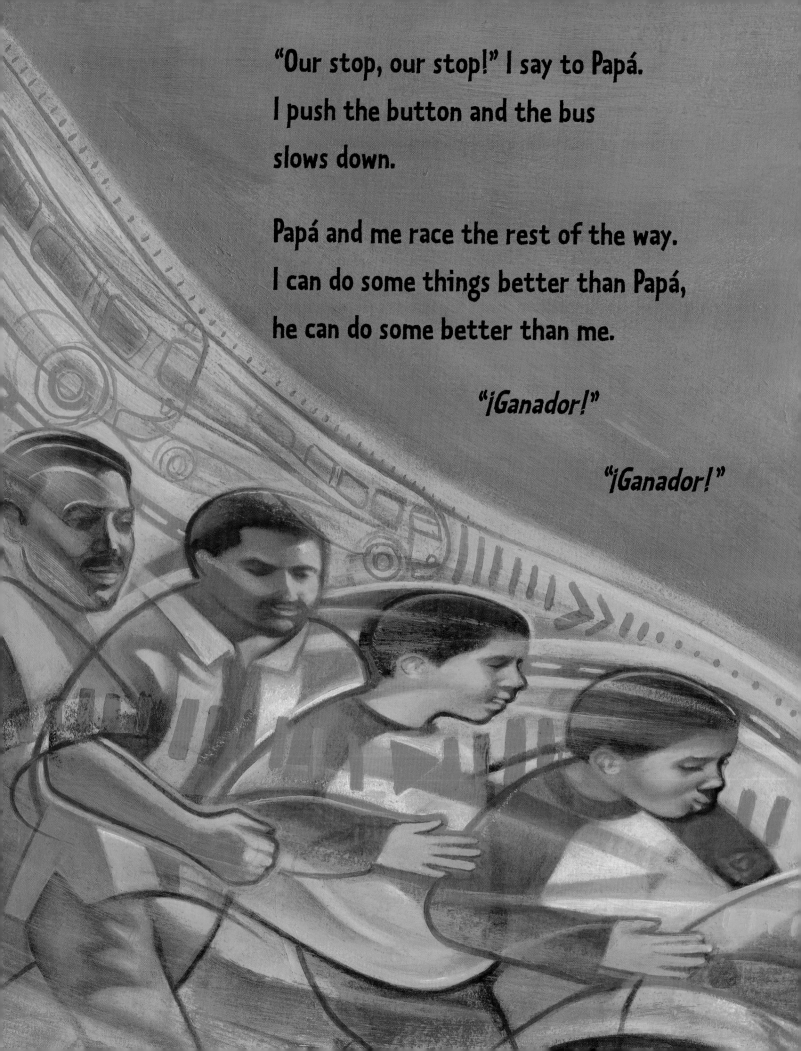

I knock on the door.

No one answers.

"*Otra vez*," Papá says.

I try again.

The door creaks open.

Abuela and Abuelo,

my grandparents,

Papá's mother and father,

are waiting for us.

"*¡Abrazos!*" They give hugs

to me and Papá.